To
Lucinda, Frances and Leo (minor) *P.M.*

Conceived and designed by
Ian Butterworth/The Artworks Press
Cover design by Vandy Ritter
Typeset in Monotype Garamond.
The paintings in this book were created using gouache on watercolor paper.
Printed in Hong Kong.

Library of Congress Cataloging in Publication Data:

Malone, Peter, 1953–
        Star shapes/ by Peter Malone.
        p. cm.
        Summary: Illustrations and rhyming text describe some of the animal constellations seen in the night sky.
        ISBN 0-8118-0726-6 (hc)
        [1. Constellations–Fiction. 2. Stars–Fiction. 3. Stories in rhyme.] I. Title.
PZ8.3.M31045St 1996
[E]–dc20   95-38256
                                                                CIP

                                                                                    AC

Distributed in Canada by
Raincoast Books
8680 Cambie Street
Vancouver B.C. V6P 6M9

10 9 8 7 6 5 4 3 2 1

Chronicle Books
85 Second Street
San Francisco, CA 94105

Web Site: www.chronbooks.com

Star Shapes

Peter Malone

chronicle books · san francisco

Night is falling. Stars are calling.

Look at the sky. What can you see?

In the twilight, brown bear growls.

In the forest, gray wolf howls.

White hare hops his moonlit dance,

while whale sleeps and dolphins prance.

Fishes swim as swan flies by.

Snake looks up with beady eye.

Proud peacock struts all in blue.

Dog stands guard all night through.

Far away, mighty lion roars.

Into the dawn, graceful eagle soars.

Then, in the sky, one by one,
the stars twinkle, fade, and are gone.

Stargazing

People have gazed up at the stars for thousands of years. They noticed that some of the stars made patterns, or constellations, in the sky. Babylonian astronomers, around the year 2000 BC, recorded these constellations, and a Chinese star map from as early as 1300 BC shows the Big Dipper.

While people in these early civilizations didn't know where stars came from, or how they were made, they did notice that the stars appeared in different parts of the sky at different times of the year. They recorded the times when the stars appeared and disappeared, and used these facts to trace the passing of months and seasons. But still people didn't know why the stars moved, or where they went when they disappeared.

To try to explain these strange, beautiful objects that shone in the night sky, people gave them names and they made up stories about them. In the year 150 AD the Greek astronomer Ptolemy produced a book which contained a list of forty-eight constellations and their Latin names. These names are still used today. We now also know that there are a total of eighty-eight constellations in the sky and that stars come in many different sizes, some shining more brightly than others.

Ptolemy believed that the Earth was the center of the universe and that the stars spun around it. Today, we know that although it looks to us as if the stars are inside a vast hollow globe that spins around the Earth once a day, it is the Earth, not the sky, that is spinning. Once astronomers understood this, they realized two things: first that stars shine even during our daytime, it's just that the light of the Sun is so bright that it hides them. Second, because the Earth's position changes as it moves around the Sun, stars appear in different parts of the sky at different times of the year, and sometimes seem to disappear altogether. Wherever you are standing on Earth, you won't be able to see all the stars and constellations because some of them are blocked by the Earth. Those that can be seen from the Earth below the equator belong to the Southern Stars; those seen from above the equator are part of the Northern Stars. The best time to look for a particular star is during the time of year when it is on the opposite side of the Earth from the Sun.

The best place to look at the stars is somewhere away from brightly lit towns and cities. This is why telescopes used by scientists and astronomers are often built on mountains. But if you pick a clear, dark night, you will be able to see hundreds of stars, and the constellations some of them make, from your own home.

The Great Bear
Latin name: *Ursa Major*
Hemisphere: Northern
Best time to see: All year round

The Great Bear is one of the oldest constellations. It has 19 stars. The seven brightest stars make up the Big Dipper.

In Greek mythology, the Great Bear was originally Callisto, beautiful maid of the goddess Hera. Callisto was so beautiful that Hera became jealous and angry. To protect Callisto, Zeus, king of the gods, turned her into a bear. Later, to save her from hunters, Zeus placed Callisto in the sky.

In ancient England this constellation was known as "King Arthur's Chariot." *Arth* means "bear" and *utheyer* "wonderful."

The Wolf
Latin name: *Lupus*
Hemisphere: Southern
Best time to see: Summer

This constellation lies in the sky next to *Centaurus*. To the ancient Greeks, the wolf was a wild animal that the Centaur carried on his spear as a sacrifice to the gods.

The Hare
Latin name: *Lepus*
Hemisphere: Northern
Best time to see: Winter

Greek legend has it that the great hunter Orion especially liked hunting hare, and so a hare was placed close to him in the sky.

The Whale, or Sea Monster
Latin name: *Cetus*
Hemisphere: Northern
Best time to see: Fall

In Greek mythology, Poseidon the sea god was angry when Queen Cassiopeia boasted that she was more beautiful than his sea nymphs. He sent a sea monster to attack Queen Cassiopeia's kingdom. The kingdom would be saved only if the Queen's daughter, Andromeda, was sacrificed to the monster. Andromeda was tied to a rock by the sea, but just as the monster was about to catch her, she was rescued by the brave hero Perseus, son of Zeus, who turned the monster to stone. That mythological monster was *Cetus*, which we today call "whale."

The Dolphin
Latin name: *Delphinus*
Hemisphere: Northern
Best time to see: Summer

The dolphin is traditionally a symbol of friendship and kindness. According to one Greek legend, the poet and musician Arion was on a sea journey when he was attacked by the ship's crew. Arion begged the sailors to let him play one last tune on his lyre. As he played, dolphins gathered around the ship. Arion suddenly jumped into the sea and one of the dolphins carried him to safety. According to this legend, it is this dolphin that you can now see in the sky. Another legend says that a dolphin helped the sea god Poseidon to find Amphitrite, the mermaid that became the god's queen. As a reward, Poseidon placed the dolphin in the sky.

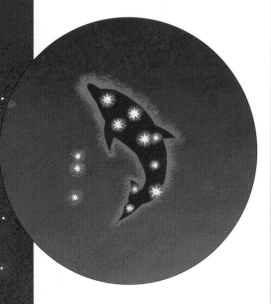

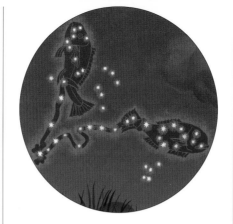

The Fishes
Latin name: *Pisces*
Hemisphere: Northern
Best time to see: Fall

In a Greek legend, the gods Aphrodite and Eros escaped from the giant Typhon by turning themselves into fishes. The goddess Athena celebrated their escape by placing two fishes in the sky.

The Swan
Latin name: *Cygnus*
Hemisphere: Northern
Best time to see: Summer

The Swan is one of the most beautiful constellations and one of the easiest to find. One Greek legend says that Cygnus was the best friend of Perseus, the son of Zeus the sun god. One day, Perseus drove his father's chariot across the sky. Worried that the chariot's heat was going to burn the earth, the other gods threw Perseus into the sea. Cygnus dove into the ocean and swam tirelessly searching for his friend. To reward his act of friendship, the gods turned Cygnus into a swan and placed him in the sky.

The Snake
Latin name: *Serpens*
Hemisphere: Northern
Best time to see: Summer

The snake is the largest constellation and appears in the sky in two parts, the head and the tail.

The Peacock
Latin name: *Pavo*
Hemisphere: Southern
Best time to see: Fall

This is one of the brightest bird constellations among the Southern Stars. If you watch its chief star for several nights, you can see it get brighter then fade again.

The Lion
Latin name: *Leo*
Hemisphere: Northern
Best time to see: Spring

The lion is often called King of the Beasts. *Leo's* brightest star is called Regulus, which means little king.

According to Greek mythology, the hero Heracles undertook 12 Labors, or tasks, for Eurystheus of Argos. His first task was to kill the Nemean Lion, which was sent from the moon by his enemy, the goddess Hera. Heracles strangled the lion with his bare hands and from then on wore the lion's skin, which made him invincible.

The Eagle
Latin name: *Aquila*
Hemisphere: Northern
Best time to see: Summer

Aquila is one of the brightest of summer constellations. One of its chief stars, Altair, is white and is easy to find because it has a paler star on either side of it.

Greek legend has it that Zeus, king of the gods, wanted a young shepherd boy, Ganymede, as a servant. He sent an eagle to bring Ganymede back to Mt. Olympus, home of the gods, and it is this eagle you can now see in the sky.

The Great Dog
Latin name: *Canis Major*
Hemisphere: Northern
Best time to see: Winter

Canis Major is easy to find because its collar contains Sirius "The Dog Star," the brightest star in the northern sky. The Great Dog is the bigger of the two dogs belonging to Orion the hunter. They follow their master across the sky, forever chasing Lepus, the hare that can be found at Orion's belt.